Ruffleclaw

Ruffleclaw

CORNELIA FUNKE

ILLUSTRATED BY THE AUTHOR

TRANSLATED BY OLIVER LATSCH

RANDOM HOUSE 🏠 NEW YORK

Text and interior illustrations copyright © 2005 by Cornelia Funke
Translation copyright © 2015 by Oliver Latsch
Cover art copyright © 2015 by Vivienne To

All rights reserved. Published in the United States by Random House
Children's Books, a division of Penguin Random House LLC, New York.
Originally published as *Zottelkralle* by Cecilie Dressler Verlag GmbH & Co.
KG, Hamburg, Germany, in 2005.

Random House and the colophon are registered trademarks of
Penguin Random House LLC.

Visit us on the Web!
randomhousekids.com

Educators and librarians, for a variety of teaching tools, visit us at
RHTeachersLibrarians.com

Library of Congress Cataloging-in-Publication Data
Funke, Cornelia Caroline, author, illustrator.
[Zottelkralle. English]
Ruffleclaw / Cornelia Funke ; illustrated by the author ; translated by
Oliver Latsch. — First American edition.
        pages cm
"Originally published as Zottelkralle by Cecilie Dressler Verlag GmbH & Co.
KG, Hamburg, Germany, in 2005" — Copyright page.
Summary: "An earth monster decides to move in with a human family"
— Provided by publisher.
ISBN 978-0-385-37548-1 (trade) — ISBN 978-0-385-37550-4 (lib. bdg.) —
ISBN 978-0-385-37551-1 (ebook)
[1. Monsters—Fiction.] I. Latsch, Oliver, translator. II. Title.
PZ7.F96624Ru 2015 [Fic]—dc23 2014025124

Printed in the United States of America

10 9 8 7 6 5 4 3 2 1

First American Edition

For the two monsters Elmar and Oliver

Ruffleclaw's burrow lay well hidden under an old toolshed, right next to Shaggystink's and Wormtooth's burrows. For its main entrance, Ruffleclaw had loosened three floorboards inside the shed. Outside, carefully hidden among high stinging nettles, was the emergency exit, because Ruffleclaw was an earth monster, and earth monsters were cautious creatures.

Like any other earth monster's burrow, Ruffleclaw's home smelled of earthworms and millipedes, but the floor was covered with soft sweaters, and piled high in the corners were all the human things he had snuck away with over time.

Ruffleclaw's neighbors, Shaggystink and Wormtooth, came to visit him only very rarely.

"Yuckity-icky-yuck!" Shaggystink moaned

every time he poked his head into Ruffleclaw's burrow, always holding his big nose with at least two of his four paws. "What a horrible stench!"

Wormtooth would just mutter something about human filth and quickly return to her own burrow, which was filled with the delicious scent of hundreds of woodlice.

Ruffleclaw didn't care at all what those two

thought. Let them munch their bugs and scratch their fleabites. Let them wallow in the mud and slurp slippery slugs. All of that was just not enough for him. Oh no.

While the other monsters spent their nights digging for hideous treats in the humans' trash cans, Ruffleclaw padded right up to the human house on his furry paws.

Oh, how those bright windows lured him closer. And the music! That horridly wonderful jingly-music. It made his knees go all wobbly.

Usually Ruffleclaw just peered through the windows, or he listened at the walls with his delicate ears. Sometimes, though, when the nights were particularly dark and when nothing moved in the human house, Ruffleclaw would open the big door and sneak inside. The silly lock was of course no problem for his monster claws.

And what exciting things they had in there! Ruffleclaw's night eyes needed no lights to spot all the wonders in the dark. He would grunt with joy as he rolled around on the thick carpets or dug his furry face into the soft pillows. He took the most delicious treats from the ice-cold box where the humans collected their food.

And at the end, he always went to look at the faces of the sleeping humans, staring in wonder at their naked, completely un-furry skin.

"Those humans look like mole rats!" Shaggy-stink said with a laugh. "Like huge, icky mole rats."

So? Ruffleclaw thought. Was their shaggy monster fur really any better? There were always lice and fleas in it. The humans probably never had to deal with *that*. And the humans didn't smell of damp earth, but of delicious soap. Yum!

Ruffleclaw had once taken a piece of soap back to his burrow and slowly eaten every last bit of it. It was the most delicious thing he'd ever tasted!

"You'll meet a terrible end one day!" Worm-tooth warned him. "You already smell like a human! Yuck!"

"And?" Ruffleclaw asked, his green eyes turning red with rage. "You'll see! Oh yes, you will!"

"See what?" his monster neighbors asked uneasily.

But Ruffleclaw just bared his teeth and grinned. His scrumptiously smart plan was none of their business.

Ruffleclaw's plan was really quite simple: he was going to move in with the humans. Indeed! After all, some of them kept cats or dogs, so why not an earth monster? Earth monsters were much smarter and way more entertaining!

The house Ruffleclaw kept sneaking into was home to three humans: two large ones and one small one. The large human with the hair on his face was hardly ever there. The other big human was a female. She seemed a little scary, because she had pieces of glass in front of her eyes. But the little human was just right.

He was only double the size of an earth monster, and he had a cozy-looking bed as well as lots of mysterious playthings. Perfect company for a slug-slimy, smart earth monster.

One night, while Wormtooth and Shaggy-

stink were already out digging for woodlice, Ruffleclaw packed a tin of worms into his bag. Earth monsters start losing their fur if they don't regularly eat worms, and Ruffleclaw had never seen any worms in the human house. Heaven only knew what they took against hair loss.

Ruffleclaw's monster heart was beating wildly as he climbed up the tunnel to his main entrance. He pushed up the floorboards and hopped onto the dusty floor of the shed. Then he nudged the boards back into place and snuck out into the dark garden.

He could hear Wormtooth and Shaggystink squabbling somewhere in the dark. Earth monsters loved to fight. Often their fights would escalate into wrestling matches, and four-armed monsters wrestling can get very wild.

They were probably fighting over some particularly juicy bug. Ruffleclaw's mouth watered at the thought, but he walked on. He had more important things to do.

Let those two spend the rest of their lives fighting over silly bugs, sitting in their smelly burrows, and freezing their scrawny tails off in winter. He, Ruffleclaw, would be lying in a warm human bed and eating human cake. Oh yes! He walked even faster toward the house.

There it was, dark and quiet. Only one faint

little light was burning above the entrance. Ruffleclaw's bendy legs clambered the three steps to the front door. He carefully poked a pointy claw into the lock. *Snap!* The door swung open. The earth monster stepped through it and listened.

Nothing. Just a faint ticking somewhere in the back. Ruffleclaw quietly closed the door and scurried to the stairs. He knew exactly where he was going.

The little human's room was on the second floor, right by the stairs. The door was always left ajar. The little human was barely visible. Only his tousled hair poked out from under the quilt. The thin curtains filtered the moonlight.

Ruffleclaw's sharp ears listened to the human's even breaths. He stood there, the bag in his hand. He suddenly felt a little uneasy. He quickly took out his tin and stuffed a half-dried worm into his mouth. Yes, that was better. Smacking his lips, he tiptoed toward the bed and crawled in next to the little human. Ah, so nice and warm! And yum! Ruffleclaw's nostrils greedily sucked in the air. There was that wonderful soap smell. He grunted happily and dug himself deeper into the soft pillows. *Oh, if Wormtooth and Shaggystink could see me now,* he thought. And then he was fast asleep.

3

The little human into whose bed Ruffleclaw had crawled was called Tommy, and Tommy woke to the sound of someone snoring next to him. It was very rhythmic and very loud snoring. Tommy pinched himself in the arm. But the snoring didn't go away.

Tommy carefully lifted his blanket. He pushed out one leg, then another, and then jumped out of the bed. He quickly flicked on the light. What he saw nearly took his breath away.

Something red and very shaggy crawled out from under the blanket. "Hey, what's going on?" the thing growled angrily. "Turn off that light right now!"

Startled, Tommy obeyed. But even with just the moonlight coming through the curtains, the horrible creature was still quite visible. It stretched four arms into the air and gave a wide-mouthed yawn that showed a frightening number of quite large teeth.

Tommy grabbed his badminton racket and held it out in front of him. "Get out of there!" he shouted. "Get out, you . . . you . . ."

The thing in his bed made a sulky face, but it showed no inclination to move. Quite the opposite, actually. The creature leaned back into Tommy's pillows and crossed two of its arms over its chest. With the other two arms, it scratched its belly.

"Now, now!" it said with a hoarse voice. "What kind of a welcome is this? Is that nice? Is that polite?"

"How did you get in here?" Tommy asked. He was still holding up his badminton racket. "What kind of a thing are you?"

"Thing? Tsk." The shaggy visitor angrily shook his head. "My name is Ruffleclaw. Try to remember that. And I am no thing. I am an earth monster."

He got up on his bowed legs and bared his teeth in a sort of smile. Then he spat against Tommy's wall—*splash!*—leaving a bright green spot on the wallpaper.

"Hey! Stop that!" Tommy cried out.

"Why? Where do you spit?" the monster asked calmly.

"I don't spit at all!" Tommy started rubbing at the stain with a tissue, but the wallpaper stayed green.

"Right. So, no spitting." The monster scratched his ear and yawned. "Got to remember that. Since I'll be living here now." And with that he dropped back into Tommy's bed.

"You'll be *what*?" Tommy lowered his badminton racket and stared at Ruffleclaw.

"Close your mouth. Makes you look kind of stupid," the earth monster observed.

Tommy just stood there in his pajamas and didn't know what to say.

"You humans have some slimaliciously awesome stuff!" The monster looked around.

"What's that there, with the buttons?"

"A radio," Tommy muttered. "You better not press tha—"

Too late. Howling guitars, booming drums. Startled, the monster howled. He grabbed the radio with two of his hairy hands and bit into it.

The sound immediately died. The monster angrily threw the dead device into a corner.

"What is that horrible thing?" the monster asked.

"That *was* my radio!" Tommy groaned. "Don't monsters like music?"

"Puh! Music? That wasn't music," the monster growled disdainfully. He hopped off the bed.

"But somewhere in this house, there's sometimes really creepy-crawlicious music!" He rolled his eyes in delight.

"My mother is a piano teacher," said Tommy, "but . . . how did you know that?"

"I've been watching you." Ruffleclaw opened Tommy's desk drawer and peered inside. He picked up a bright green eraser and plopped it into his mouth.

"Not bad. You eat this stuff often?"

"We never eat this stuff!" Tommy slammed the drawer shut. "Leave my things alone."

"Oh, don't be such a grouch!" Ruffleclaw grunted. Then he spat again, this time on the carpet. "Earth monsters can't stand grouchiness. Got that?" Ruffleclaw waddled back to the bed. He reached for the dirty bag he'd left on Tommy's nightstand and pulled out a tin.

"Nevertheless, little human"—the earth monster fished something out of the tin, something that looked suspiciously like a dried earthworm—"I like it here. Despite your

constant griping." And with that, the worm disappeared into his wide mouth.

Tommy was feeling sick. "Yuck. What are you eating?" he asked.

"Worms." The monster smacked his lips. "Why? Want one? They'd be even better with some snail slime."

"No thanks," Tommy muttered.

"Since we're talking food"—Ruffleclaw patted his belly—"I wouldn't mind some seconds from your icebox."

"So you already know our fridge!" Tommy groaned. "This can't be real. It just can't." He squeezed his eyes shut and opened them again.

The earth monster was still there. He was just closing his vile tin. Then he crawled back under Tommy's blanket and burped. Tommy stood shivering in front of his own bed.

"And?" Twenty hairy fingers started impatiently drumming the blanket. "Where's the food? Huh?"

Tommy put on his bathrobe and opened the door.

"See ya!" Ruffleclaw shouted after him.

"See ya!" Tommy mumbled. He looked at the door to his parents' bedroom. His dad was away. As usual. Tommy's dad was a travel guide. But his mom was there. *And?* Tommy thought. *What am I going to tell her? That there's a red worm-eating monster in my bed?*

Tommy sighed and went down the stairs. *Never mind*, he thought. *I always wanted a dog, and now I have a monster.*

4

The next morning, Tommy's alarm went off at six-thirty, and the earth monster was gone.

There was no filthy bag on the nightstand, nor was there any other trace of his presence. *So it was only a dream after all,* Tommy thought. But he wasn't sure whether he should be glad about that or not.

He padded sleepily to the bathroom and nearly ran into his mom.

"Where did you come from?" she asked. "I thought you were in the shower."

"No, why?" Tommy rubbed his eyes.

"Then who's that in the bathroom?" Mom asked. "Your dad is touring through some desert thousands of miles from here."

Tommy stared at the closed bathroom door. Very slowly his brain started to catch on to who was taking a shower in there.

"I . . . erm . . . am letting the water run until it's hot."

"Ah," Mom said. "Let's not make that a habit, okay? And hurry up, please."

"Sure." Tommy quickly disappeared into the bathroom and locked the door behind him.

The earth monster was standing under the shower. Soaking wet. Soap bubbles all over his chin.

"Have you gone completely crazy?" Tommy hissed. "Get out of there right now."

"Wouldn't dream of it!" Ruffleclaw purred. "Ahhh, this feels good! And it tickles. Snail-slimifyingly good!"

Tommy picked up the empty shampoo bottle from the floor.

"Did you pour all that over your head?"

"Mousepoop! I'm not as crazy as you think." With a huff, Ruffleclaw turned his back on Tommy. "I drank most of it, of course."

"Yuck!" Tommy yanked the tap shut. He

pulled the struggling monster out of the shower and pressed a towel into his claws. "There. Dry off. And be quiet. My mother's up."

"Just as well!" the monster grunted as he gave the towel a nosy sniff. "You can introduce us."

"Introduce you? Are you insane? I'm hiding you."

"Why?" Ruffleclaw pouted and spat into the sink.

"Because she would give you to the zoo, or have you stuffed, or something worse," Tommy whispered.

That sounded unpleasant. Very unpleasant. The monster uneasily scratched his belly.

"Tommy? What are you doing in there?" his mother called through the door.

"Almost done!" Tommy shouted back. He quickly threw another big towel over Ruffleclaw's head. "Keep still, if you want to live," he whispered as he tucked the twitching bundle under his arm.

"My tin! My tin!" Ruffleclaw shrieked.

Tommy found the filthy bag under the sink. He stuffed it into his towel-bundle and opened the bathroom door.

"Where are you going with my towel?" his mother called after him.

"To dry myself, of course!" Tommy answered. Then he quickly disappeared into his room.

Enraged, Ruffleclaw wiggled out of the damp towel. "I don't like that!" he hissed. "Oh no!" He grabbed the towel and tore it to shreds.

"Be quiet, you idiot!" Tommy hissed back. "My parents can't stand animals. And my dad's allergic to everything."

"I'm not an animal!" Ruffleclaw growled. "I am an earth monster."

"Even worse!" Tommy quickly climbed into his pants and pulled a T-shirt over his head. "You better hide under the bed or . . . hold on . . . yes, the closet is probably more comfortable. I'll be back in the afternoon."

"What?" the monster screamed. "What are

you talking about? I'm supposed to hide in that smelly closet there? That's boring. I might as well have stayed in my burrow."

"And why didn't you?" Tommy screamed back. "I didn't invite you."

Ruffleclaw spat precisely right in front of Tommy's naked feet. "Typical human!" he grumbled. "But all right! I'll go into that smelly closet . . . *if* I get something to eat."

"I'll get you something." Tommy opened the closet. "Now get in."

"Fine!" With a dark face, the monster climbed into his prison. "Disgusting!" he muttered, but Tommy just slammed the door shut.

5

The breakfast Tommy threw into the closet before he disappeared was delicious, absolutely delicious. But in return, Ruffleclaw had to promise again to stay put. The monster licked his claws and chuckled quietly. What a pity that earth monsters never kept their promises. Never. Ever. He burped and patted his belly. Then he gave the closet door a good kick. *Slam!* — it banged open, and bright daylight hit his eyes. Mousepoop! The light had already bothered him when he woke up. But if he wanted to stay with the humans he'd better learn to live with it. They always slept through the night and ran around in the horrible sunlight. Gross.

His eyes screwed up against the sun, Ruffleclaw leapt out of the closet. Ah, at least the windows had curtains. Once he pulled those shut, his eyes began to feel better. What now? Ruffle-claw scratched his fur and thought. Should he go back to the room where the water came out of the ceiling? No, he'd done that already.

"I'll have a quick look around!" Ruffleclaw whispered to himself. "There's enough to see in here."

First he pulled all the boxes from Tommy's shelves and with his four arms poked around all his toys. The dice and the playing cards looked particularly interesting. The cards didn't taste too bad, but the dice felt a little heavy in his stomach.

Smacking his lips, Ruffleclaw climbed up to the fourth shelf. It was full of wheeled thingies. The ones that didn't smell of anything got kicked off the shelf right away. The others he collected in his arms, and he crash-landed on Tommy's bed with them.

He got a few minutes of fun out of chewing on the things and their rubber wheels, but then Ruffleclaw looked around for something new to do. He ate some of the colorful pens on Tommy's desk and pressed a few of the many buttons on a flat box without anything happening. Then he began to feel bored.

Somehow these human things weren't half as exciting as Ruffleclaw had thought. Disappointed, he went to the door and pressed his ear against it. But he couldn't even hear any of the gruesomely beautiful jingly-music he'd listened to from the outside on so many evenings.

Fine. That left only one thing to do.

Ruffleclaw took one big leap back into Tommy's bed. He pulled the quilt over his head. Ahhh! The earth monster groaned with joy. That was more like it. Yes! Ruffleclaw yawned—and nearly swallowed his tongue with shock.

There were steps coming up the stairs. Heavy steps. From a big human, at least three times his own size. No! Five times. Ten times!

Panicked, Ruffleclaw looked around. Should he go back into the closet? No, too late. The steps were coming closer. And closer. Ruffleclaw's thoughts raced around in his head like a swarm of angry bees.

The door opened. Ruffleclaw disappeared under the covers. He listened. But his ears couldn't hear much under the thick blankets.

"Oh no!" he heard someone sigh. "What's this mess? I can't believe it. Tommy! Come up here, now!"

Tommy? Was he back already?

Someone pulled open the curtains, knocked into the bed, and lifted the quilt. Ruffleclaw quickly squeezed his eyes shut. *Play dead,* he thought. Playing dead was always good.

"Yuck!" Tommy's mother cried. "Where did you get that horrid stuffed animal? Did your dad give that to you?"

"What—what stuffed animal?" Ruffleclaw heard Tommy stutter.

"That one there! The red thing with the four arms."

"Oh, that. Yeah, Dad brought that back from Madagascar or somewhere."

"Goodness! Why can't your father bring back something pretty for a change? No, it's always one tasteless and crude thing or another."

Tommy's mother angrily plucked away at Ruffleclaw's fur. "Ugh, feels horrible. Tommy, you will throw that thing away, understood?"

Now it was Ruffleclaw's turn to get angry. He got so angry that he nearly jumped up to call Tommy's mother a slimy slug to her face.

"But . . . I actually like it," said Tommy.

His mother sighed. "Fine! I have to practice now. Food's on the stove. Oh, and clean up this infernal mess."

Bam! The door fell shut, and Tommy was alone with his monster.

6

"How mean!" Ruffleclaw was biting into Tommy's pillow. "That horrible slug. Oh, she'll pay for that. She will!"

"No, she won't!" Tommy angrily kicked at the crumpled boxes on his floor. "What were you thinking, huh? At least half of these are ruined!"

"Puh!" the monster growled. He picked a flea from his ear and squashed it with a pop.

"You promised to stay in the closet!"

"Promised—puh. So what?" Ruffleclaw spat on Tommy's lamp, then pricked his ears. "Hey. Quiet!"

There it was! The monster rolled his eyes with delight. "Ahhh!" he grunted. "Oh! Jingly-music! Creepy-crawly wondermusic. Ooooh!"

He quickly hopped off the bed and ran to the door to listen.

"Is that music coming from the wall?" he asked impatiently. "Or from one of those buttony machines? Tell me, tell me!"

"That? That's just my mom." Tommy angrily tossed the chewed-up crayons into his wastebasket.

"Your mom?" Ruffleclaw opened the door. "That horrible slime-slug can make such bugalicious music? Nah!"

"She's practicing the piano, you thickhead. And stop calling her a slug!" Tommy was checking over his favorite toy car. All four wheels had been bitten off.

"Look at that!" Tommy shouted. He shook the car accusingly in Ruffleclaw's direction, but all he saw was a tail disappearing through the door.

"Hey! Stop!" Tommy tried to dive for the tail, but he just crash-landed, empty-handed, on the floor. The monster was already rushing down the stairs and toward the music as if in a trance.

"Oh no!" Tommy groaned. He took a few hair-raising leaps down the stairs. The monster was standing in the living room doorway, humming like a bumblebee, waving his four arms, and shaking his hairy backside. Luckily, Tommy's mother was facing the other way.

Tommy didn't stop to think. He grabbed one of his mom's huge shopping bags, snuck up behind Ruffleclaw, and quickly pulled the bag over the monster. The hairy head, belly, arms, and legs disappeared, and only the feet still poked out from under the bag. Ruffleclaw hissed like an angry cat, but he couldn't free himself.

Tommy quickly turned the bag, stuffed the furry feet inside, and squeezed the bag shut. His mother kept playing — she never heard anything when she was practicing.

Tommy dragged the heavy bag to the stairs and lugged it up the steps. By the fifth step, Ruffleclaw had already bitten through the bag.

By the time Tommy reached his room, two hairy arms were trying to grab hold of his face, the sharp claws only narrowly missing his nose. "Let me out!" Tommy heard the monster's muffled hiss.

Completely out of breath, Tommy threw the bag on top of all his broken toys and slammed the door shut.

Ruffleclaw clawed his way out of what was left of the shopping bag. He jumped on Tommy and started pummeling him with his four red paws.

"Ouch!" Tommy screamed. "Stop it! Are you crazy?"

"I want to hear that music, you sneaky slime-face!" the monster ranted. "I want, I want, I want!" Then he angrily stomped his crooked legs.

"You should be glad my mother didn't see you! I saved your life, that's what I did. We slime-slugs, we love to put things like you in cages, or, even better, stuff them and put them

in a museum. How often do I have to tell you that?"

Ruffleclaw dropped his fists and spat half-heartedly into the corner. Then he clambered onto Tommy's bed and disappeared under the quilt.

"Get out of there!" Tommy said. "You're helping me clean up. Now!"

"Can't. Headache," Ruffleclaw groaned. "I can't handle all this stupid daylight."

"If that's your problem"—Tommy rummaged through his desk drawers—"here!" He pulled the covers off the monster and dropped a pair of sunglasses onto his belly. "Put these on."

Ruffleclaw eyed the strange contraption. Then he gave them a sniff and put them on his head.

"Not like that!" Tommy snickered. He put the glasses on Ruffleclaw's monster nose. "There. They fit perfectly. Only your ears are in the wrong place."

"What? My ears are in the perfect place!" Ruffleclaw walked off to study his reflection in the mirror on Tommy's door. "Slimalicious!" was his verdict.

"Fine!" Tommy impatiently dragged him away from the mirror. "But now it's cleanup time, or there won't be any more food."

That finally did it.

7

Ruffleclaw slept through the rest of the day. After all, daytime was his usual sleep time. And on top of that, life with the humans was quite exhausting. Much more exhausting than he'd imagined.

And so he slept, gulped down an earthworm or two, slept a little more, ate a mountain of salami sandwiches, including the plate, and slept. Tommy couldn't believe the laziness. A few times he tried to shake the monster awake, because the snoring was disrupting his homework.

"Wow, I always thought monsters were wild and obnoxious," he muttered. "But you just lie around and stuff yourself. Are you sure you're a monster and not some kind of sloth?"

"What mousepoopy nonsense!" Ruffleclaw growled groggily. "All monsters are like this. Lazy, hungry, and greedy—that's us." He plopped another earthworm into his mouth, spat against the ceiling, and went back to sleep.

Maybe a dog would be better, Tommy thought. He cast a bored glance at the shrunken head his father had brought back from his last trip. Where had he gone this time? Ah yes, the Sahara. So he was probably going to bring back a camel candleholder or a pyramid-shaped saltshaker. Tommy chuckled as he rolled the shrunken head over his desk.

"Tommy!" his mother called from downstairs. "Come down, please. You have to go shopping with me."

"Why?" Tommy quickly kicked the shredded shopping bag under the desk.

"Because your father's coming back tomorrow. Or have you forgotten that?"

Tomorrow? Already? Tommy groaned. There was his next problem: Dad's allergies were definitely going to give Ruffleclaw away. It was going to be a nonstop sneeze fest.

"Hurry, please!" Mom called. "And have you seen my big shopping bag anywhere?"

"No!" Tommy shot an angry look at his bed, where Ruffleclaw was lying all lazy and peaceful. His fur was full of crumbs. *I should stop worrying about the monster,* Tommy thought. *That sloth can take care of himself. I'd rather have a dog anyway.* So Tommy went downstairs to go shopping with his mom—without her favorite shopping bag, which had mysteriously disappeared.

The silence woke Ruffleclaw up. No complaining human, no jingly-music, no steps. Nothing. He looked around the empty room. Then he went to the top of the stairs and listened. Still nothing.

Gone, he thought. *Just gone. Without saying a word. How rude!* Ruffleclaw peered over the banister. On the other hand, this was not so bad. At least he'd get to look around in peace. He hopped down the stairs and ran straight

into the kitchen. Ah yes, the icebox. The little human was too stingy with his food portions. Ruffleclaw gave his belly a worried look. Too thin. Time to do something about that. He greedily opened the icebox.

Oh, what creepy-crawlicious delicacies! Ruffleclaw helped himself. The sausages in one hand, the eggs in another. The third hand grabbed the cake and the fourth the honey jar. That should do it for now. He kicked the icebox shut. Then he dragged his loot to the magical chest that made the jingly-music.

He put the food on the shiny black lid and

climbed onto the stool Tommy's mom had sat on. With two paws, he stroked the white and black keys—leaving him with exactly ten claws to stuff some cake into his mouth. Ruffleclaw carefully pushed down one of the keys. *Pling!* His eyes rolled with joy, and he let out a happy burp.

His next attempt was bolder. *Pling! Pling! Pling!* The jingly-music bubbled from under his furry fingers.

Ruffleclaw was ecstatic. So ecstatic that he threw the sausages and the cake on the carpet behind him and started hitting the keys with all four paws. Oh, this was true slimalicious bliss, totally creepy-crawladocious! His clawed fingers raced up and down and across the keyboard. Ruffleclaw nearly fell off the stool with delight. He quickly opened the honey jar, dipped one paw after another into it, and licked them. One claw went back into the jar, while the others stickily continued plinking away at the keyboard. Suddenly he heard voices through the front door. Ruffleclaw dropped the honey jar.

"Where's that key?" he heard the slug ask.

They were back. Huge wormadocious bummer. Why did they have to interrupt him now? Ruffleclaw angrily hopped off the stool. He quickly gathered the remains of his picnic and crawled under the overstuffed red couch.

8

Heavy human feet came stomping into the house. The noise they made! Incredible. Ruffleclaw bit another chunk off the sausage and listened.

"Put it all on the kitchen table!" the slug called. Then Ruffleclaw heard her open the icebox. Oops.

"Tommy?" she asked. "Did you eat the sausages?"

Nope, he did not! Ruffleclaw thought. He suppressed a giggle as he stuffed the last bit of sausage into his mouth.

"And the cake!" The slug sounded amazed. "The cake's gone, too!"

And the cheese, thought Ruffleclaw. His belly felt wonderful. Perfectly full and round. He let out a tiny burp.

"I—erm—I was really hungry," he heard Tommy stammer.

"You ate all that? Boy, you'll probably be ill!" the slug cried out. "And that trail of dirt there. That was you as well?"

"Probably," said Tommy, though he didn't sound very convincing.

"It goes all the way to the living room!" Now the slug began to sound worried.

High, pointy shoes came clicking into the room, followed by Tommy's squelching sneakers. Ruffleclaw couldn't make out more than that through the tassels of the couch.

Suddenly Tommy's mother uttered a piercing scream, making the monster hit his head against the bottom of the couch.

"Oh! My piano!" she moaned. "Crumbs, splatter, and . . . spittle?" She touched the keys. "My fingers! They are sticking to the keyboard! And this was your work, too, Tommy?"

"Me? I—I don't quite remember," Tommy stuttered.

Ruffleclaw was beginning to feel a little uneasy in his hiding place.

"What's going on here?" the nasty slug asked. Her pointy shoe kicked the empty honey jar, which lay on the carpet less than a foot from where Ruffleclaw was hiding. Blast! He'd forgotten about that one. He pricked his ears as he gulped down the rest of the cake. For a long while, there was nothing but torturous silence. Then the nasty slug spoke with a low, threatening voice. "There are hairs on the piano stool. Sticky, smelly red hairs. Tommy? What is going on here? Spit it out!"

But Tommy said nothing. Ruffleclaw snarled quietly, but he also shuffled a bit farther under the sofa.

More silence.

"And what is that?" Tommy's mother asked suddenly.

What is what? Ruffleclaw thought. His eyes were fixed on the pointy shoes, which were coming closer and closer.

"That!" the slug shouted out in triumph as she grabbed Ruffleclaw's tail.

He tried to hold on to the legs of the couch, but Tommy's mother yanked his tail so hard that he howled in pain and let go. His wonderful, slimalicious sunglasses slipped off his nose, and the sun pierced his eyes.

That was too much.

Growling, Ruffleclaw spun around, jerked his tail free, and jumped to his feet. Hissing through his bared teeth, he lunged at the big pale slug.

"Help!" Tommy's mother screeched. She quickly scrambled on top of the piano. Ruffleclaw went after her, and the hunt continued over the stuffed chairs, the little tables, and finally onto a chest of drawers, which toppled under their combined weight. Mother and monster rolled across the carpet.

"You vile vermin!" Tommy's mother howled as she smashed a big vase on his head.

"Slimy slug!" Ruffleclaw howled back, spitting on her blouse.

"Just you wait!" Tommy's mother panted as she struggled to her feet and ran to the wall that was covered from floor to ceiling with souvenirs from her husband's travels.

"Mom, no!" Tommy shouted, but his mother already gripped the long spear his dad had brought back from some African trip.

Ruffleclaw was so startled, he started to hiccup. An earth monster wasn't defeated very easily, but that thing the slug was waving around in front of his nose looked dangerous. Ruffleclaw decided to run for his life, past Tommy, who sat frozen in a puddle of honey.

"Traitor!" Ruffleclaw hissed as he ran past him, and he spat on his nose for good measure. Then he ran out into the corridor and toward the front door. Tommy's mother came after him, jabbing the horrid spear in his direction, her hair poking out in every which way, her eyes wide and crazy.

With less than a second to spare, the lock sprang open, and Ruffleclaw dashed outside, cursing madly as he flew down the front steps. "You horrible, treacherous slugs! You slithery, bug-eyed ..." And with that, he disappeared into the shrubs.

Tommy's mother, spear in hand, appeared in the doorway. She looked around. She continued looking for a few endless moments while Ruffleclaw made faces at her from under the shrubs. Finally she went back into the house, and the door slammed shut.

9

With his body and soul hurting badly, Ruffleclaw peered out from under the greenery.

"What a shame!" he growled. "What a
sludgy, slimy shame!"

And, even worse, there was not even the tiniest bit of food to be had for him. The tin with
his precious stash of worms was out of reach.
Muttering curses, Ruffleclaw scratched his aching tail. What now? The shed and his burrow
were endless monster-meters away. How was he
supposed to get there in broad daylight without
that crazed slug skewering him with that spear?
Ruffleclaw knew there was only one thing he
could do: he had to dig a tunnel to his burrow.
But he really, really didn't want to.

Splash! A huge raindrop landed on his nose.
And another. And another. Ruffleclaw groaned.

Not that as well! He hated rain nearly as much as he hated digging tunnels. Digging was hard work, and he was a lazy monster. But what else could he do?

Growling, cursing, and spitting, Ruffleclaw went to work. And soon there was only a hole and a small mound of dirt where he'd been sitting.

Ruffleclaw dug and dug and cursed the humans, those horrible, big humans, who grabbed their monster guests by the tails and ran them out of the house with spears. Those treacherous, little humans, who wouldn't help their monster friend, just because he'd made a bit of a mess. So sneaky! So cowardly! Dog-fartily, cat-scratchily nasty — that's what they were.

At least Ruffleclaw ran into a few worms on his endless dig, and with every one he ate, he felt a tiny bit better.

But then he had to think of the little human again, who had done absolutely nothing to help him against that nasty slug. And again Ruffleclaw wanted to bite a hole into his own fur.

When he finally broke through into his burrow, Ruffleclaw's four arms ached and his empty stomach growled, but he let out a big sigh of relief. He lay down on his bed of soft sweaters.

Humans are disgusting, he thought. *But some of their stuff is still slimaliciously wonderful.*

A spider was slowly descending from the earth ceiling, but Ruffleclaw was too tired to eat it.

He curled up with a weary grunt and immediately fell asleep.

"See? I was right," Wormtooth whispered. "He's back. And he's gotten quite fat."

Ruffleclaw opened his eyes and saw his two neighbors standing by his bed. "Hey, Ruffleclaw," said Shaggystink. "Where've you been? We thought the dog had gotten you."

Ruffleclaw sat up and yawned. "I was in the house of the humans," he said, scratching his belly.

"The human house?" Dumbfounded, his earth monster neighbors looked at each other.

Wormtooth was the first to regain her speech. "Can't have been too bad," she said, patting Ruffleclaw's belly.

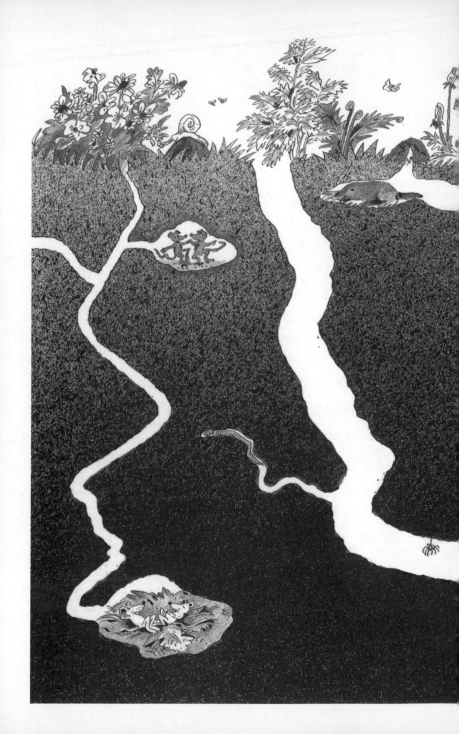

"It was wonderful," Ruffleclaw bragged. "But then it got a bit boring. And I was running out of worms."

Shaggystink sniffed Ruffleclaw's fur and wrinkled his nose. "Yuck! You smell horribly of soap."

"I drank a whole bottle!" Ruffleclaw happily rolled his eyes at the memory. "Ooooh, it was creepy-crawliciously yummy. Bugalociously wonderful!"

The other two shuddered.

"Well, you're obviously just as crazy as before," said Wormtooth. "Want to come over for some pill bugs? I can't bear the stink in here anymore."

"Yes! You have to tell us what that house is like," said Shaggystink. "And I'll bring some worms to nibble on."

"If you insist," Ruffleclaw replied generously. "You go ahead. I'll be along in a little while."

He sat in his burrow, pondering. The dim

light soothed his eyes, and he breathed in the delicious smells of pill bugs and centipedes.

It's nice to be home, Ruffleclaw thought. But then he sighed. He was going to miss Tommy's bed. And the cake. And the jingly-music. Oh, that heavenly jingly-music.

10

Tommy was sad. Miserable.

Yes, he had to admit, Ruffleclaw had been quite a pest. Always hungry. Always tired. And he spat absolutely everywhere. And still ... Tommy missed him.

Now he was alone again.

He'd cleaned Mom's piano and the carpet. The spear he'd taken to the attic. And then he started planning how he could get Ruffleclaw back.

Finding him was not the problem. The monster had told him where his burrow was: under the old shed. Getting him to come back should also not be too difficult. A little cake and chocolate would do the trick. But ... Mom. Mom was a problem. And Tommy didn't even want to start thinking about Dad. *First things first,* he thought.

First he had to convince Mom that he would get sick if he didn't get Ruffleclaw back. Very sick. Then he had to make her feel guilty for nearly skewering the monster, although Ruffleclaw had only growled and spat a little. Mom was very easy to guilt-trip.

He tried the same trick he'd once used to get out of a math exam. With Mom's face powder, he made himself look as pale as a zombie. Then he tottered down the stairs and collapsed on the couch, near where Mom was dusting Dad's travel souvenirs.

"Goodness! Your face!" she cried out. "You're not getting sick, are you?"

Tommy made his best near-death face and nodded. "Yes. Unless I get Ruffleclaw back."

"Ruffleclaw? Is that what that monster is called?" Mom asked. "Impossible! Just so it can devour us all in the middle of the night? You can't be serious."

"He's totally harmless," said Tommy. "Really. He just acts dangerous. Cats also hiss and show their claws."

"I can't stand cats," his mother replied. She rearranged an ivory Eiffel Tower and two plaster Greek goddesses. "But their claws aren't that long. And they don't stink."

"You frightened him to death," said Tommy. "Otherwise he would never have gone after you."

"Really? *I* scared *him* to death?" his mother shrieked. "And what about me? A four-armed monster chases me onto my own piano, spits at me, scratches my legs, and *I* am supposed to have scared *him* to death? Ha!"

"I'll get him to stop spitting," Tommy mumbled. "You have my word. And we could trim his claws a little."

"No way!" his mother said. "That's final. Period. The end. Go watch some TV. That'll take your mind off this nonsense."

"No," said Tommy. "I want my monster back."

"You can have pancakes for dinner."

"I'll only eat when I get my monster back."

"That is simply not an option!" his mother hissed angrily.

Tommy crossed his arms. "I'm officially on hunger strike. And I won't go to school, either. Final. The end."

"But that's just silly," his mother whined. She was fiddling with her earlobes, something she only did when she was nervous.

"The last time you acted up like this was when Dad brought you that horrid sailor costume," she said angrily. "You remember? He asked you to wear it to school. Back then I could understand your reaction. But now?" She shook her head. "All this drama because of that horrible creature?"

Tommy stared at the carpet and said nothing.

"Oh, come on," his mom said. She got some licorice sticks and put them in front of Tommy. "Maybe you can have a guinea pig or a bird. Dad's not allergic to those, is he?"

"But I want my monster!" Tommy insisted. He ignored the licorice, which was terribly hard. Then he sighed a very deep sigh and dragged himself up the stairs to his room.

A short while later, his mother knocked on

his door. "Come on, Tommy!" she said. "A monster as a pet? One morning we'll wake up to him nibbling on us."

"Ruffleclaw doesn't eat humans. He's nice!" Tommy replied. "Lazy, yes, and greedy, but nice. And you went after him with a spear. Just because he spilled something on your piano."

"He looked dangerous," Tommy's mother said angrily. "With all those arms and teeth. Well, never mind. I have to practice."

And she was gone.

Tommy listened intently to the sounds coming from downstairs. His mother missed at least every third note. *There we go!* He quickly dashed to the bathroom to put some more powder on his face.

Ten minutes later, his mother poked her head through the door again. "You heard it—I can't even practice, just because you're such a stubborn boy. Please be reasonable now."

"I want my monster back," said Tommy.

"But that's completely crazy!" his mother

cried. "I know you've always wanted a dog, but a monster . . ."

"I don't want a dog, I want a monster!" Tommy said. "And I'll train him. Promise!"

Tommy thought, *Now is the time to play your trump card.* "He loves your piano playing, Mom!" he said. "He goes all gooey listening to it. Really."

"What? That thing?" His mother blushed, just like she always did when someone complimented her playing. "Nonsense."

"But it's true!" Tommy added. "That's why he was all over the piano. He wanted to make beautiful music like you do. Couldn't you teach him? Just imagine, he could play four-handed all by himself."

Mom's piano-teacher eyes started glowing. But then she shook her head again. "No way, this is ridiculous. That horrible, disgusting creature . . ."

"He loves to bathe," said Tommy. "Oh, please, Mom. Please, please let me have my monster."

"Impossible. What's your dad going to say?"

Tommy grinned. "Dad loves disgusting things."

"Well . . . maybe . . . but that creature's long gone now anyway."

And that's when Tommy knew he'd won.

11

Ruffleclaw returned from Wormtooth's burrow in an excellent mood. How those two had stared at him as he told them of his adventures in the house of the humans. They'd gone green with envy, yes, bright green. Of course he hadn't told them about the less pleasant incidents. And why should he have?

Smacking his lips with joy, Ruffleclaw crawled into his pile of sweaters and closed his eyes for some well-earned sleep.

But he'd barely been snoring for five minutes when he heard strange, scraping sounds right above his head. As if something was crawling across the floor of the shed. What was that now? Hadn't he had enough excitement in the past days? Worried, he pricked his ears. Maybe a cat? Or a dog?

"Hey, Ruffleclaw!" a familiar voice suddenly called. "Are you there?"

It was the human named Tommy! What was he doing? Ruffleclaw's fur stood on end.

And now the boy was knocking on the floorboards. Intolerable! Growling with rage, Ruffleclaw crawled up the tunnel and pushed away the floorboards at the top.

"What do you want?" he hissed. "Go away! I don't want anything to do with you. Nothing!"

The little human made a sheepish face. On the floor next to him stood a large basket from which some very tempting smells wafted into Ruffleclaw's sensitive nose.

"I'm very sorry!" said Tommy. "Really! Very sorry! But why did you have to make such a huge mess? And right on Mom's piano?"

"Puh!" Ruffleclaw's wide mouth screwed up with disdain. "She nearly skewered me! Yes, skewered! And she almost ripped off my tail. And then I had to dig a tunnel under the entire garden to get home. My arms are still aching.

I don't even want to think how many years of
my life all of that has cost me."

Tommy reached into his pocket. "Here. I
brought you your sunglasses. And look!" He

pushed the basket right in front of Ruffleclaw's big monster nose. "This is for you."

"Hmph." Scowling, Ruffleclaw grabbed the sunglasses. Then he hopped out of his hole and peered into the basket.

"Sausages," said Tommy, "and cookies. And eggs. You like eggs, don't you?"

"And cake?" Ruffleclaw's four hands rummaged through the basket. "No cake?"

"You already ate all the cake!" Tommy called out. "You can be glad I still found this stuff in the fridge."

Ruffleclaw just grunted. He snatched the basket and was about to shove it into his tunnel when Tommy grabbed his arm. "Hey, wait a minute," he said. "I brought this so you'd come back."

"What? Back? With you?" the monster shrieked—without letting go of the basket, of course. "Do you think I have a death wish or something?"

And suddenly the little human looked very

sad. "Please?" he said. "Please come back. You won't have to sit in the closet anymore. And I've hidden the spear in the attic. On my honor."

"Hmm." Ruffleclaw reached into the basket and popped an egg into his mouth. Yum! The shell crunched wonderfully between his teeth. "What about that nasty slug?" he mumbled, rubbing his injured tail.

"My mother wants to teach you to play the piano," said Tommy.

Now Ruffleclaw was speechless. "Jingly-music?" he breathed.

"Yes, exactly. Jingly-music!" Tommy nodded. "I told her that pupils with four hands are quite rare."

"Ha!" Ruffleclaw frowned and scratched his ears. Then he scratched his belly, and then his nose. Finally he grinned. He grinned from one pointy ear to the other. "Sold! Yes. You convinced me."

He peered down his tunnel. Then he pushed the basket toward Tommy. "You take that," he whispered. "Let's get out of here."

"Why are you whispering?" Tommy asked.

"Because of the others!" Ruffleclaw pulled the floorboards back into place. Then he waved Tommy to follow him as he tiptoed toward the door. "Can't you make your fat human feet walk a bit more quietly?" he hissed angrily.

Tommy tried. "What others?"

"My neighbors," Ruffleclaw grunted. "Wormtooth and Shaggystink. Two earth monsters, just like me, only not as nice, and not half as smart."

"Ahhh!" Tommy whispered. He looked around, but he couldn't see any sign of more earth monsters. "And why shouldn't they hear us? I'd like to meet them."

"Puh!" Ruffleclaw pushed the sunglasses onto his nose and pointed at the basket. "So they can eat all this yummy stuff? No way! Anyway, they're always squabbling and fighting. Disgusting."

Ruffleclaw didn't mention that he also liked

to do those things from time to time. Instead, he quickly pattered down the flagstone path toward the house.

Tommy took the basket and followed the monster—past all the plaster statues, totem poles, and Eiffel Towers his father had planted all over the garden. Ruffleclaw stopped in front of the ugliest of the totem poles.

"This is what made me move in under your shed," he said. "Nobody else has such freakalicious stuff in their yards."

The pole had always given Tommy the creeps. Only a monster could like a hideous thing like that.

They both continued toward the house.

"Oh, and don't mention earthworms when Mom's around," Tommy said as he unlocked the door. "Just tell her how wonderful her piano playing is and stuff like that."

"Got it!" said Ruffleclaw. "And I probably shouldn't call her slug, either, right?"

"Unless you do want to get skewered after all!"

"Puh!" Ruffleclaw spat into the grass.

"And stop doing that, too, okay?" said Tommy. "No more spitting."

"Yes, yes, yes, yes!" the monster grunted. "And what about her? I hope she's not going to behave like such a human all the time or make stupid comments about my fur. I won't be able to control myself."

This is going to be interesting, Tommy thought as he pushed the door open.

12

Tommy's mother was just giving a lesson as they walked into the house.

"Phwerk!" Ruffleclaw muttered. "What kind of horrible noise is that?"

"Come on," said Tommy, pushing him toward the stairs. "First you're going to take a shower."

"No problem!" Ruffleclaw grunted. "But only if I get another bottle of that yummy shampoo."

"Fine!" Tommy shoved the monster through the bathroom doorway. "But don't drink it all, okay? Use some for washing as well. You're smelling kind of funky."

"Moany, moany, moan!" Ruffleclaw answered. "Have I said a word about your horrible human smell? And that soap stuff is way too precious for washing."

"Just do what you want with it," said Tommy. He threw a bottle of shampoo into the shower and went back to his room.

Tommy lay down on his bed and started plotting how he could get his dad into a monster-agreeable mood. Not even the strongest shampoo would help with Dad's allergies, even if Ruffleclaw decided to use at least some to wash himself.

By the time Mom walked her pupil to the door, Tommy still hadn't come up with a plan. With a sigh he went back to the bathroom—and couldn't believe his eyes.

A dripping-wet Ruffleclaw was standing in front of the mirror, using Mom's lipstick to paint pink spots onto his fur.

He was singing, "Pling! Plong! Jingly-jingle!" and beginning to paint his nose as well.

"Oh no!" Tommy groaned. "What are you doing?"

Ruffleclaw grinned proudly at his reflection in the mirror. "Slimalicious, isn't it?" His dripping paws reached for Tommy's mother's favorite perfume.

"No!" Tommy shouted. "Don't touch that!"

"Why?" Ruffleclaw gave the little bottle a blissful sniff. "Creepy-crawliciously, wormaliciously wonderful! Please? Just one tiny sip?"

"No!" Tommy quickly took the bottle from Ruffleclaw's paw. "Don't touch this, unless you want to have another fight with my mother. It's not for drinking anyway."

"No?"

"No, it's for spraying onto your skin."

Ruffleclaw scratched his wet belly. "What a waste!" he grunted.

Tommy also took the lipstick from him, though there wasn't much left of it. Then he took his mom's hair dryer from the cabinet.

"What is that?" Ruffleclaw asked warily. When Tommy switched it on, the monster bared his fangs and retreated into a corner.

"Stop that!" said Tommy. "This is for drying your fur."

Ruffleclaw kept his back turned to Tommy, but when he felt the warm air on his fur he started to gurgle with delight. "Ooooh! Warm wind from a can! Wormalicious!"

It took quite a long time to dry the entire monster. Ruffleclaw just couldn't get enough of it, and he complained bitterly when Tommy turned off the hair dryer. Ruffleclaw moaned and scratched his fur, which was still covered with pink lipstick.

"Stop moaning and come on!" Tommy said. He opened the bathroom door. "My mother's probably waiting already."

"You think?" Ruffleclaw nervously poked a claw into his ear. "I think I need another earthworm first."

"No," said Tommy. "Come on."

Ruffleclaw started whining, "But worms are good for the nerves!"

"Not for my nerves," Tommy retorted, pulling the monster toward the stairs.

The first minutes in the dining room were horrible. Even though there was more cake. Tommy's mother and Ruffleclaw stared at each other across the beautifully laid table. Tommy wriggled on his chair and watched the two with

growing panic. His mother looked as if she was going to jump up at any minute. The knife she'd used to cut the cake was lying right next to her hand.

Ruffleclaw, in turn, looked as though he knew she was going to jump up and skewer him. He didn't even look at the cake. His nose kept nervously sniffing the air.

"Would you like some cake, Ruffleclaw?" Tommy asked into the silence.

The monster pursed his lips, and for a terribly long moment Tommy thought he was going to spit on the table.

But then the monster just warbled, "Yes, please! Thank you."

Like the perfect monster, he folded two of his claws over his belly and used the other two to reach for his cup.

He slurped his coffee a bit too noisily, and there was just the tiniest burp afterward, but he did manage to nibble his cake quite tidily.

One of Tommy's mother's eyebrows went up

with surprise. This was a good sign. Relieved, Tommy helped himself to a piece of cake.

"Ahhh!" Ruffleclaw sighed, rolling his eyes. "A creepy-crawlicious cake."

"I'm sorry?" asked Tommy's mom.

"Oh, that's just a monster expression, Mom!" Tommy said quickly while he kicked Ruffleclaw under the table.

The monster gave him a startled look. Then he turned to Tommy's mother and gave her a grin so wide that she could see all his teeth. Through them he mumbled, "I would love to hear some of the snail-slimalicious jingly-music now."

"Oh!" said Tommy's mother.

Nothing else. Just: oh. But her cheeks turned as red as cherries.

Tommy squeezed his eyes shut and braced himself for the explosion. *Here we go,* he thought. But then he heard his mother laugh. A little awkwardly, but she laughed.

"Is your hairy friend asking me to play the piano?" she asked.

"He, erm, yes—yes, that's it!" Tommy stuttered. "He's crazy about your playing. He just can't say it very well."

"Oh!" his mother said again. She rose with an angelic smile and floated to her piano stool.

Tommy knew what was coming, and he couldn't suppress a yawn. Ruffleclaw, however, sat perfectly still and pricked his ears. No burps, no grunts, no growls—nothing. Tommy's mother played and played, and eventually the monster started to sway happily from side to side. He hummed a little, and a couple of times he smacked his lips.

Oh boy, Tommy thought as he stuffed himself with cake. *I hope she doesn't keep going for the whole afternoon.*

Finally Tommy's mother lifted her hands from the keyboard and gave a little bow. She always did that after playing.

"Wormaliciously wonderful!" Ruffleclaw cried. "So bug-slime, slugociously amazing!" He clapped with all four paws and nearly toppled into the cake with enthusiasm.

Tommy's mother turned as red as a radish.

"I told him you'd teach him," said Tommy.

Ruffleclaw stared down at his paws.

"Well . . ." Tommy's mother cleared her throat. "And . . . why not?"

Quick as lightning, the monster was off his chair and hopping next to her onto the piano stool. His grin could not have gotten any wider. He lifted his hairy paws and went for it. His claws zipped up and down and across the keyboard.

Astonished, Tommy's mother stared at the four red paws. Ruffleclaw's playing sounded a little strange, but it did sound a little bit like what Tommy's mother had just played.

"Wonderful!" Tommy's mother exclaimed when Ruffleclaw finally dropped his paws. "Absolutely wonderful! You're a natural! A four-handed natural, no less." She lovingly patted the monster's shaggy head. "What a talent. My dear friend, I am so sorry for how I treated you before."

"Oh, let's just forget about that!" Ruffleclaw
grunted, scratching his belly. "But now I could
really do with another piece of cake, couldn't
you?"

When it had long been pitch-dark outside,
Tommy's mother and Ruffleclaw were still playing piano—six handed. Tommy slept on the sofa
and dreamed of piano-playing monsters.

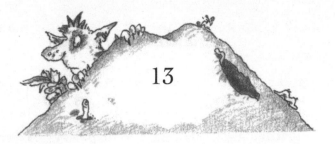

13

They went to bed at midnight, but just a couple of hours later, Ruffleclaw shook Tommy awake.

"Don't tell me you're hungry!" Tommy muttered sleepily. "You ate at least six pieces of cake."

"I heard something!" Ruffleclaw hissed. "Downstairs, by the front door."

Tommy sat up. "I don't hear anything."

"Puh! Human ears!" Ruffleclaw grunted. He hopped out of the bed and ran to the door. "I know who that is. It must be one of the others!" he muttered. "But there's not space here for more than one earth monster. Oh no! I'm going to have to drive them away!"

And with that, he was gone.

"Hey, Ruffleclaw, wait!" Tommy crawled out of bed and yawned. "What are you talking about? What if it's a burglar?" He padded to the stairs.

And then he heard it, too: someone was fiddling with the front door lock.

"Ruffleclaw!" Tommy whispered. "Come back!"

"No way. Just let them come in!" he heard the monster growl in the darkness.

"Where are you?" Tommy hissed.

He heard a suppressed curse from outside the door. Suddenly the lock snapped open.

Tommy cowered behind the banister.

The door opened slowly. A long shadow stretched into the corridor. A human shadow.

The figure took a step through the doorway — and was immediately jumped by Ruffleclaw.

Hissing and growling, the monster held on to the intruder's neck, pummeled him with his fists, spat in his face, and pulled his hair.

"Help!" the intruder cried. "Help me!"

Tommy knew that voice.

"Dad!" he screamed. "Ruffleclaw! Let him go. That's my dad!"

"What?" Ruffleclaw croaked. He dropped to the ground like a sack of potatoes.

The lights flashed on, and Tommy's mother appeared at the top of the stairs. "What on earth is going on?" she asked. Then she spotted her husband.

"What are you doing here already? I thought you were arriving tomorrow morning! And why are you sitting on the floor?"

"I got an earlier flight." Tommy's father was rubbing his neck. "And I'm sitting on the floor because my legs have gone a little wobbly." He sneezed twice. "Could someone please explain to me what that is?" He pointed at Ruffleclaw, who had collapsed in a corner.

"That is my monster," Tommy answered sheepishly.

"Your what?"

"His monster," said Tommy's mom. "His name is Ruffleclaw, and he can play the piano — with four hands."

"Is that so?" Dad sneezed again — five times.

"And he loves your totem poles!" Tommy added quickly.

Ruffleclaw finally found his voice. "Oh yes! Those are bugtastic!" He got up and walked with outstretched paws toward Tommy's dad.

His dad, however, jumped up, tried to take a step back, and fell over his suitcases. Cursing, he picked himself up, now rubbing his neck and his head, and started sneezing again.

"Watch it there!" Ruffleclaw grinned at Tommy's dad. He was still holding out his paw. "Welcome!" he grunted. "Glad to finally see a slug with at least a bit of hair on the face."

"What?" Tommy's dad touched his beard — and sneezed again. "I'm sorry," he sniveled, taking the monster's red paw. "But I'm allergic to animal hair."

"Oh, that's fine. I don't mind," replied Ruffleclaw.

"Well, I kind of do." Tommy's dad sneezed some more, this time so hard that the vase by the entrance toppled over and spilled its water all over his shoes.

Tommy and his mother exchanged a quick, helpless look.

"Ah, bit of a sensitive nose there?" Ruffleclaw observed. He bent down and mopped up the water from Dad's shoes with his paws. "That is indeed slimaliciously annoying. I had that once with cats. Always made me sneeze like a trumpet."

Tommy's dad sneezed—seven times this time. Ruffleclaw looked at him full of sympathy.

"We could shave his fur, Dad," Tommy called. "But please let me keep him, okay?"

Ruffleclaw shot Tommy an angry look. "What? Shave? This is my fur you're talking about. My snail-slimaliciously, awesome fur!" He bared his fangs. "There won't be any shaving—and you should be glad if *I* decide to keep *you*, you little slug."

Tommy's dad chuckled, which immediately led to another sneeze. His nose was dripping like a leaky faucet. "I'm sorry," he croaked. "You really are a funny fellow, Scuttleclaws, or whatever you're called." Three more sneezes. "But, as you can see, I really can't have any fur in the house." Four short and three long sneezes.

"Nonsense!" Ruffleclaw grunted. He sniffed eagerly at Tommy's dad's luggage. "There're plenty of good recipes against itchy noses."

Tommy's dad rubbed his red nose. "For example?"

Ruffleclaw scratched his belly. "For example, two earthworms wrapped in a spiderweb. You just have to chew thoroughly, but it helps right away."

Tommy's father looked disgusted and sneezed six times.

"Or"—Ruffleclaw continued—"you keep
these in your pocket." He plucked off three
hairs from his tail and handed them to Tommy's
father. "But you have to spit on them first."

Tommy's father eyed the monster hairs in-
credulously, but then he spat on them and put
them in his pocket.

Everyone looked at him, except for Ruffleclaw, who was poking the luggage that was still
standing in the open door.

"Well? Dad?" Tommy asked. "How are you feeling?"

His father touched his nose and smiled.

"It's not itchy anymore!" he called out. "Not even a tiny bit. It worked!"

"Of course it worked." Ruffleclaw tried to peer through the suitcases' zippers. "Earth monster remedies always work. And what's in these?"

Tommy's dad was still prodding his nose. "Oh, those are my clothes, probably some desert sand, and a few souvenirs."

Tommy and his mother rolled their eyes, but Ruffleclaw excitedly bounced from one paw to the other. "Open them, open them!" he grunted. "Are those things as super-slimalicious as the other stuff you've got standing around here?"

Tommy's father let go of his nose and beamed. Nobody had been this excited about his souvenirs in years.

"Hold on," he said eagerly. "I'll show them to you." He took one suitcase and the monster took the other, and together they disappeared into the living room.

Tommy stared after them from behind the banister.

"Tommy, I believe you can keep your monster," his mother said.

Tommy grinned. *Now I just have to make him understand that those souvenirs are not for eating,* he thought.

And then he went up to his room to lie on his bed and wait for his monster.

The next day, Tommy said to Ruffleclaw, "Now that you're living here, don't you want to invite your monster friends over?"

"Stupid idea!" Ruffleclaw grunted. It was afternoon, and he was lying on Tommy's bed, the almost-empty worm tin next to him.

"Why? We could get lots of cake and have a really nice monster tea party. What's stupid about that?"

"Firstly, I'd rather eat the cake myself," Ruffleclaw growled. "And, secondly, they would never dare to come here anyway."

"Oh, come on," said Tommy "I'd love to meet them."

"No!" Ruffleclaw barked.

"Just think how much you could brag to them!" said Tommy. "You can show them the bathroom, and the fridge, and all the soft beds."

"Hmm." Ruffleclaw poked a claw into his left ear. That did sound fun. "But then I need two more pairs of sunglasses. They won't come without sunglasses."

"No problem," replied Tommy.

"Fine!" Ruffleclaw grunted. He pulled the quilt under his chin. "But don't say I didn't warn you."

Wormtooth and Shaggystink accepted the invitation, mainly because of the sunglasses.

Tommy's mother wrinkled her nose just a little bit as the two grinning monsters came hopping through the front door. The two of them did smell rather strongly of pill bugs and centipedes, but she tried to overlook that for friends of Ruffleclaw. She even shook their paws, though they were a little sticky and slimy.

When Wormtooth and Shaggystink came into the living room, Ruffleclaw was already sitting at the piano. He thought he'd impress his

friends, but the two brutes just sat down next to him and swatted at the keys a few times.

Tommy's mother started to twitch nervously, but they very quickly lost interest and made for the coffee table.

They hopped on the sofa, wallowed on the knitted pillows, reached with their greedy paws for the cake, and by the time Tommy's parents warily sat down on their chairs, anything edible—along with a few inedible things—had disappeared from the table.

Shaggystink and Wormtooth rolled around on the sofa, grunting happily and licking their sticky paws.

"So this is how slugs live?" Wormtooth asked between two long burps. She put her smelly feet on the coffee table.

"What?" Tommy's mother tried to hold her nose without anyone noticing. "What slugs?"

The reply came in the form of double monster howls of laughter.

"Well, this hole would give even crawlies the creeps!" Shaggystink growled. He picked a flea from his fur and cracked it between his teeth.

Tommy's parents were shocked, and Ruffleclaw was satisfied. His two neighbors would definitely not receive another invite to eat his cake. Oh no.

The only one who seemed to enjoy Wormtooth's and Shaggystink's burping and grunting was Tommy. He even asked them whether he

could visit them in their burrows. Ruffleclaw's
ears went green with envy.

"Sure, you can visit us," Wormtooth hissed.
"We might even rustle up some slithery-fresh
earthworms for you!"

"Yes, and moldy bread!" Shaggystink rolled
his eyes with delight. "Moldy bread is the best,
but it has to be all green through and through.
Never could figure out why you slugs throw
that stuff out."

Tommy's face went as green as bread mold.

"Hey, nakedface!" Wormtooth croaked. "Let
me feel your skin." She hopped onto the table
and over the plates and cups and touched Tommy's cheek with her sticky paw.

"Amazing!" Giggling, Wormtooth jumped off the table and grabbed hold of the lamp. She dangled above their heads and continued, "They even feel like slugs. For real! Do you taste like slugs, too?"

Tommy's parents stared up at the dangling monster with wide-open mouths.

"Come on, Wormtooth!" Shaggystink suddenly croaked. He jumped off the sofa and muttered, "After all this, I need some decent worms."

Wormtooth let go and landed right next to her friend.

"Have fun, Ruffleclaw!" they both grunted. Then the two monsters spat in unison on the carpet and ran out of the room. The front door slammed shut just a moment later.

15

"Heavens! How hideous!" Tommy's mother groaned. "Such outrageous behavior. Are those two really your friends, Ruffleclaw?"

"Nah, no way!" Ruffleclaw grunted dismissively. "Just neighbors. You can't always pick your neighbors, can you?"

"That smell!" Tommy's mother sighed.

"And look at that!" Tommy's father pointed at the tablecloth. "They even tried to eat that. My dear Ruffleclaw, I am very sorry, but those two will not be welcome here again."

"No problem!" Ruffleclaw replied. Of course he didn't mention that it was he who'd nibbled on the tablecloth. "I never wanted to invite them. That was Tommy's idea."

"Really?" Tommy's mother looked at him.

"Yes!" Tommy said stubbornly. "And I don't think they were that bad."

"Puh!" Ruffleclaw turned his back to him. "I'm going to sleep!" he growled, and disappeared upstairs.

When Tommy came up, Ruffleclaw didn't speak a word to him. He just took his worm tin and went to the window.

Tommy was putting on his pajamas. "Where are you going?" he asked.

Ruffleclaw pouted and opened the window. "Out!"

"Hey, wait a minute!" Tommy said. "I was only joking down there. I thought those two were awful. You're much nicer."

"Hmm," Ruffleclaw grunted. He jumped on the windowsill.

"Come down from there!" Tommy cried. "What are you doing? You're going to break your neck!"

"Mousepoop!" Ruffleclaw countered. "I'll climb down the gutter. Simple."

"But why?" Tommy asked. He grabbed one of the monster's arms. "Fine! I won't go and visit them. I won't eat their worms or their moldy bread. On my honor!"

"As if I care!" Ruffleclaw pulled his arm away and jumped to the gutter. He clung to it like a red furry monkey. "And I have no idea what you think I'm doing. I'm just going out to get some fresh earthworms. Or is that no longer allowed?"

"So you're coming back?" Tommy asked carefully.

"Sure!" Ruffleclaw giggled. He began to climb down the gutter. "What did you think?"

Tommy sighed with relief.

"Ha! Got you there, didn't I?" Ruffleclaw howled with joy, flashing Tommy a huge grin.

"You know, you should really try to quit the earthworms. And the spitting. But we could maybe go to your burrow sometime."

"Mousepoop!" Ruffleclaw shouted back. "Where's the fun in that?"

And he disappeared into the darkness.

And Tommy? Tommy didn't sleep a wink until his monster returned.

ABOUT THE AUTHOR

CORNELIA FUNKE is the *New York Times* bestselling author of many magical books for children, including *The Thief Lord*, *Dragon Rider*, and *Inkheart*. She was named one of the 100 most influential people by *Time* magazine in 2005. She was born in Germany and lives with her family in California.

Ahoy! Set sail on another chapter-book adventure by CORNELIA FUNKE:

Who needs a treasure map when you have a pirate pig with a nose for gold?

Available now!

Take off on a magical journey with this charming chapter book by CORNELIA FUNKE:

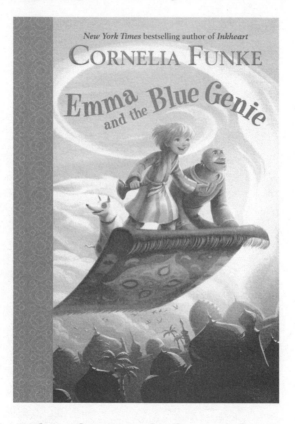

What if a genie had no wishes?
It's up to Emma and her noodle-tailed
dog to help him get his magic back!

Available now!